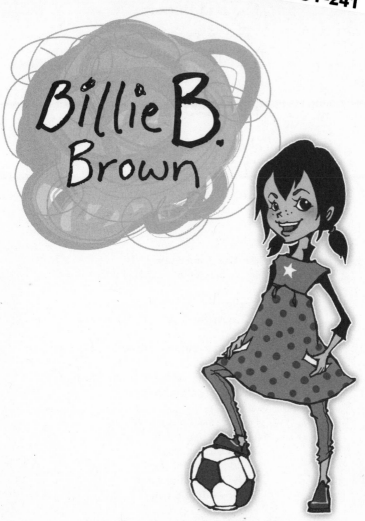

Billie B. Brown

Billie B. Brown Books

The Bad Butterfly
The Soccer Star
The Midnight Feast

Hey Jack! Books

The Crazy Cousins
The Scary Solo
The Winning Goal

First American Edition 2012
Kane Miller, A Division of EDC Publishing

Text Copyright © 2010 Sally Rippin
Illustrations Copyright © 2010 Aki Fukuoka

First published in Australia in 2010 by Hardie Grant Egmont

For information contact:
Kane Miller, A Division of EDC Publishing
P.O. Box 470663
Tulsa, OK 74147-0663
www.kanemiller.com
www.edcpub.com

Library of Congress Control Number: 2011935666

Printed and bound in the United States of America
1 2 3 4 5 6 7 8 9 10
ISBN: 978-1-61067-096-8

The
Soccer
Star

By Sally Rippin

Illustrated by Aki Fukuoka

Kane Miller
A DIVISION OF EDC PUBLISHING

Chapter One

Billie B. Brown has fifteen freckles, six pairs of stripy socks and one banana sandwich. Do you know what the "B" in Billie B. Brown is for?

Brave.

Sometimes Billie B. Brown has to be very brave. Today is one of those days.

Billie has a best friend. His name is Jack.

Billie and Jack are in the same class at school.

Banana
Sandwich

Stripy Socks

Every lunchtime they
play on the monkey bars
together. Billie hangs
upside down.

Jack swings from one
side to the other.
Then they climb to the
top to eat their lunch.

They can see the whole
playground from there.
It is a good place to eat
lunch.

Today a boy from
their grade runs over.
His name is Sam.
Sam stands under the
monkey bars and looks
up at Billie and Jack.

6

"We need another soccer player," he says.

"OK," Billie says. She looks at Jack. "Let's go!"

"Um, no girls," Sam says.

Billie frowns. "Why not?" she asks.

"Girls can't play soccer," Sam says.

Billie has never heard of such a silly thing.

"Rubbish," she says. "Anyway, I don't want to play. Soccer is a stupid game."

"Really?" says Jack. "You're a fast runner, Billie. I bet you'd be good at soccer!"

But Billie shakes her head.

She wants to tell Jack not to go and play. She wants to tell him that if he goes, she'll be left all alone on the monkey bars without her best friend.

But Billie feels too **shy** and too **cross**.

When she opens her
mouth, nothing comes out.

"You coming?" Sam says
to Jack.

"Sure," says Jack. "Want
to come and watch, Billie?"

"No," says Billie. "I told
you, soccer is boring."

So Jack swings down
to the ground.

Then he and Sam jog

over to the soccer field.

Billie sits by herself

on the monkey bars.

She still has half a

banana sandwich left in

her lunchbox. Banana

sandwiches are her

favorite, but Billie doesn't

feel hungry anymore.

The **cross** feeling and
the **sad** feeling have
muddled up her tummy.
She closes her lunchbox
and waits for the bell
to ring.

Chapter Two

When the bell rings,

Billie waits for Jack

by the drinking fountain.

She sees him walking

with the soccer boys.

He looks very happy.

"Hey, Billie," Jack says.

"We won the game!
I kicked a goal! You
should have seen me!"

Billie looks at Jack's big
smile. He has a gap in his

teeth that
makes him
look funny.
Billie laughs.

She isn't feeling so cross anymore.

"Cool!" she says. "Let's go. We are starting our project today."

"I am going to sit with Benny and Sam," says Jack. "We are going to make a soccer field. Come and sit with us!"

"Billie can't make a soccer field," says Sam.

"Why not?" says Billie.

"Because you're a girl," says Benny. "Girls don't play soccer."

Now Billie is mad again. She feels **cross** with Sam. She feels **cross** with Benny.

But most of all she
feels **cross** with Jack.
Jack is her best friend!
They always sit together.

"I don't want to sit
with you boys anyway,"
she says. "I don't want
to make a soccer field.
Soccer is boring!"

Billie's tummy starts to
feel **jumbled up** again.
She walks quickly away
from the boys. She is
worried that she might cry.

She scrunches up her face and her hands until the feeling goes away.

Ella and Tracey walk past. Ella and Tracey are best friends. They always do their hair the same way.

Billie likes Ella and Tracey, but she doesn't like doing her hair like them.

"Hey, Billie," says Ella. "What are you making for your project?"

"I don't know," says Billie.

"We're making a circus," says Tracey.

"Cool," says Billie.

"Can I be in your group?"

"Sure," says Tracey. "But what about Jack? Don't you want to sit with him? You always sit with him."

"He only wants to play with the soccer boys now," says Billie. "Sam and Benny say girls can't play soccer."

"They are right," says Ella. "Who wants to play soccer? Yuck!"

"Yeah," says Tracey. "Soccer is for boys."

"That's just silly!" says Billie. "Girls can play soccer too!"

Suddenly Billie doesn't feel sad.

She doesn't feel bad, and she doesn't even feel mad.

Billie B. Brown has an idea!

Chapter Three

After school, Jack and his mom are waiting for Billie at the gate. Billie always walks home with Jack because they live right next door to each other.

"Hi, Billie," Jack's mom says. "So, did you two have a good day at school?"

"Yeah!" says Jack. "I played soccer. I kicked the winning goal!"

"That's great," says Jack's mom. She takes their hands to cross the road. "What about you, Billie? Did you play too?"

"No," says Billie. "I didn't want to."

"That doesn't sound like you, Billie," Jack's mom laughs. "You and Jack do everything together!"

Billie takes a big breath. She feels **nervous**.

Sometimes you have to be very brave to tell the truth. It can feel scary. But today Billie has decided to be brave.

"I didn't like it when you played soccer without me," she says to Jack. "Don't you want to be my friend anymore?"

Jack looks surprised. "Of course I want to be your friend! You're my best friend, Billie! I thought you didn't want to play with *me*!"

Billie feels glad that Jack is still her friend. She was worried that maybe now he would only want to play with the boys.

Billie grins. "I have an idea. But I'll need your help. Come to the park with me when we get home?"

Jack looks at his mom.

She nods and smiles.
"Sure, I can take you kids
to the park," she says.
"Billie, you'd better go and
ask your mom. We'll meet
you out in front of your
place in ten minutes."

"OK!" says Billie.

Jack smiles. He can see
that Billie has had one of
her super-dooper ideas.

"What are we doing?"
he asks.

"I'll explain
at the park,"
says Billie.

"Bring your soccer ball.
And your red cap!"

Chapter Four

The next day, Billie's dad walks Billie and Jack to school. Sam is waiting for Jack in the playground.

"Hey, Jack," says Sam. "Playing soccer at lunch?"

"Yep!" says Jack. He looks at Billie. They grin.

In class Billie and Jack sit together, as normal. But when the bell goes for lunch, Jack runs outside with Sam. Billie stays behind.

What do you think Billie
and Jack are up to?

Jack and Sam eat their
lunch in the shade.
Then they run over to
the field. The other team
is already there.

"Hey, look!" says Jack.
"The other team has a
new player!"

The new player is
wearing a red cap and
red stripy socks.

They start the game.

Sam plays hard. Benny plays
hard. Jack plays the hardest
of all. But they are no
match for the other team.

The new player on the other team is good. Sam and Jack and Benny are fast, but the new player is even faster.

The new player runs past the boys and kicks the ball into the goal.

Everybody **cheers**!
But not Sam and Benny.
They are feeling **worried**.

The other team is winning!

"Their new player is fast!"
says Sam to Benny.

"He sure is," says Benny.

"We don't have anyone that fast on our team!"

Benny and Sam run as hard as they can. But they can't catch the new player in the red cap and stripy socks!

Soon the bell rings. The other team has won! Benny and Sam look cross. But Jack looks happy.

"Why are you smiling?"
Benny says. "We lost!"

"It's unfair!" Sam says. "Their
new player is too good!"

"Yeah," says Benny.
"Who is he anyway?"

"Come and see," says Jack.

They walk up to the
player with the red cap
and stripy socks.

The player takes off her
cap and smiles.

Do you know who it is?

It's Billie!

Sam and Benny are amazed.

"You see?" says Billie. "Girls *can* play soccer. Jack showed me how."

A boy from Billie's team walks over. "Jack was right," he says to Billie. "You *are* fast!"

"I told you!" says Jack.

"She's a Soccer Star!"

Billie looks at Sam and Benny. "Maybe I'll play on your team one day," she says.

"Um, OK," say Sam and Benny at the same time.

Billie smiles. "But only if I can be captain!" she says.

44